Whispers of the Heart

YourTimeless Writer

Ukiyoto Publishing

All global publishing rights are held by

Ukiyoto Publishing

Published in 2024

Content Copyright © YourTimeless Writer
ISBN 9789361721816
*All rights reserved.
No part of this publication may be reproduced,
transmitted, or stored in a retrieval system, in any form
by any means, electronic, mechanical, photocopying,
recording or otherwise, without the prior permission of
the publisher.*

The moral rights of the authors have been asserted.

*This is a work of fiction. Names, characters, businesses,
places, events, locales, and incidents are either the
products of the author's imagination or used in a fictitious
manner. Any resemblance to actual persons, living or
dead, or actual events is purely coincidental.*

*This book is sold subject to the condition that it shall not by
way of trade or otherwise, be lent, resold, hired out or
otherwise circulated, without the publisher's prior
consent, in any form of binding or cover other than that in
which it is published.*

www.ukiyoto.com

This book is dedicated to my other half and to the LGBTQIA+ Community.

Contents

THE ENCOUNTER	1
BRUSHSTROKES OF AFFECTIONED	3
UNVEILING EMOTIONS	6
CONFESSION IN THE RAIN	9
NAVIGATING LOVE'S LANDSCAPE	12
DANCING UNDER THE MOONLIGHT	15
DANCING UNDER THE MOONLIGHT	18
EPHEMERAL ETERNITY	21
About the Author	24

THE ENCOUNTER

In the heart of Veridian, a city that buzzed with life and whispered promises, Alex found solace in the quiet corners of his bookstore, "Whispers of the Page." It was a haven of stories, a sanctuary where the scent of old books mingled with the soft murmur of turning pages.

Riley, on the other hand, was a burst of energy in the city's vibrant art scene. His studio, adorned with canvases that spilled emotions in every stroke, stood as a testament to his boundless creativity. He was known for his vivacity, his laughter echoing through the narrow streets whenever he set up his easel.

Their worlds collided on a drizzly Tuesday afternoon. Alex, lost in the poetry of a classic novel, felt a tap on his shoulder. Startled, he looked up to find Riley standing there, a charming smile playing on his lips.

"Excuse me, you dropped this," Riley said, holding out a bookmark that had slipped from Alex's book.

Their eyes met, and in that moment, Veridian seemed to hold its breath. The silence between them was pregnant with possibility, and as Riley returned the forgotten bookmark, their fingers brushed — a fleeting touch that sent a shiver down Alex's spine.

"Thanks," Alex managed to say, a hint of blush coloring his cheeks.

"No problem at all. I'm Riley," he grinned, the twinkle in his eyes impossible to ignore.

"I'm Alex," he replied, the simplicity of his name sounding different when spoken by Riley.

Their conversation unfolded naturally, like a dance of words in a coffee-scented atmosphere. Riley's enthusiasm for life clashed beautifully with Alex's reserved nature. They spoke of books, art, and dreams that lingered in the city air.

As the day waned and Veridian's lights began to twinkle, Alex found himself captivated by the vibrant artist who had entered his quiet world. Riley, in turn, felt an unexplainable connection with the bookstore owner who seemed to hold stories not just within the pages of books but within his very being.

The encounter, seemingly ordinary, left an indelible mark on both of them. Little did they know that this chance meeting would unravel a story of love, self-discovery, and the beautiful chaos that accompanies the whispering promise of a city that never slept.

BRUSHSTROKES OF AFFECTIONED

Days turned into weeks, and the connection between Alex and Riley deepened. The quiet charm of "Whispers of the Page" became a haven where Riley's laughter blended seamlessly with the soft rustle of pages turning.

Riley's presence brought color to Alex's monochrome world. Together, they explored Veridian's hidden gems – from tucked-away cafes to secluded parks. Each moment felt like a brushstroke on the canvas of their growing friendship.

One afternoon, as they sat beneath the sprawling branches of the city's oldest oak tree, Riley shared stories behind his vibrant paintings. Each stroke, he explained, held a piece of his soul, a part of him he hadn't dared to reveal to many.

"I've always admired artists," Alex confessed, his gaze fixed on the ever-shifting leaves above. "Their ability to express what words often fail to convey."

Riley, touched by the sincerity in Alex's voice, leaned in closer. "Art has a language of its own, but sometimes, words add a depth that colors alone can't capture."

In the warmth of that shared moment, Alex found himself drawn to the hues of Riley's world. The subtle blush on his cheeks, the way his eyes sparkled when he spoke about his art – it all added layers to the canvas of their connection.

As their friendship blossomed, so did the unspoken question lingering between them. Riley, with his open heart, wondered if the connection they shared could be more than friendship. Meanwhile, Alex, with his quiet introspection, questioned whether he was ready to embrace a love that felt both unexpected and inevitable.

One evening, surrounded by the soft glow of city lights, they stumbled upon a street musician playing a melodic tune. The music became a backdrop to their unspoken feelings. Riley, unable to contain the emotions bubbling within him, looked at Alex with a vulnerability that mirrored the exposed canvas in his studio.

"Alex," he began, his voice carrying a whisper of uncertainty, "I feel something more than friendship. Do you?"

Alex, his heart echoing with a mixture of fear and longing, met Riley's gaze. In that moment, beneath the starlit Veridian sky, they stood on the precipice of something new, something that would paint their lives with the brushstrokes of affection.

UNVEILING EMOTIONS

Under the starlit Veridian sky, Alex hesitated for a brief moment that felt like an eternity. The soft melody from the street musician surrounded them, creating a cocoon of intimacy. In the quiet pause, the city seemed to hold its breath, waiting for their next move.

Riley's eyes, filled with a mixture of hope and vulnerability, searched Alex's face for a sign. The weight of unspoken emotions hung in the air, a delicate balance between friendship and something deeper.

Taking a deep breath, Alex finally spoke, his voice a gentle undertone in the melody of the night. "Riley, I've never felt a connection like this before. It's... new, and I'm trying to understand."

Riley nodded, a small smile playing on his lips. "Understanding takes time. Let's navigate this together, step by step."

Their tentative conversation unfolded beneath the twinkling stars, and with each shared revelation, the distance between them seemed to melt away. Riley shared stories of past loves and heartbreaks, while Alex opened up about the guarded chambers of his heart.

As the night deepened, they strolled through Veridian's quiet streets, their words weaving a tapestry of shared dreams and vulnerabilities. The city became a silent witness to the blooming connection, the uncharted territory of love revealing itself with every step.

Days turned into weeks, and their friendship evolved into a delicate dance. Alex, despite his reservations, found comfort in Riley's vibrant presence. Riley, in turn, admired the strength in Alex's quiet resilience.

One evening, as they stood on the balcony of Riley's studio overlooking the city skyline, a shared sense of understanding settled between them. The transition from friends to something more felt like a natural progression, guided by the gentle rhythm of Veridian's heartbeat.

Their relationship, though budding with affection, remained a secret shared between them. Veridian, with its ever-changing lights and anonymous faces, provided a safe space for their emotions to flourish.

Yet, in the shadows of the city, rumors whispered. The art community buzzed with speculation, and as the news of Riley and Alex's evolving connection spread, the delicate balance they had carefully maintained started to waver.

Caught in the whirlwind of gossip and unspoken truths, Alex found himself facing a new challenge — not just understanding his own emotions but also navigating the judgments of a city that had become an unwitting spectator to their love story.

CONFESSION IN THE RAIN

Veridian, usually bustling with life, seemed to hush into a quiet symphony as rumors of Riley and Alex's connection echoed through the city's streets. The walls that once sheltered their blossoming love story now held the weight of judgmental whispers.

Caught in the crossfire of speculation, Alex grappled with a storm of emotions. He found solace in the familiar refuge of his bookstore, "Whispers of the Page," where the scent of old books offered a sense of grounding amidst the turmoil.

One rainy afternoon, the city draped in a soft mist, Alex and Riley sought refuge beneath the same oak tree where their journey had begun. The raindrops, like confessions from the sky, added a poetic backdrop to the emotional tempest that brewed within them.

"I never expected our connection to be met with such scrutiny," Alex admitted, his gaze fixed on the rain-kissed leaves.

Riley, brushing a rain-soaked strand of hair from his face, sighed. "Veridian can be both enchanting and unforgiving. But our love is ours, Alex, and no rumor can tarnish that."

The weight of unspoken words hung heavy between them. As they sat in the quiet intimacy of the rain, Riley took Alex's hand, their fingers intertwining like the delicate dance of water droplets on leaves.

"I won't let the city's whispers drown out what we have," Riley declared, his voice firm with conviction. "Let's face it together, Alex. Our love deserves to be celebrated, not hidden."

Encouraged by Riley's unwavering support, Alex felt a surge of courage. The rain, once perceived as a metaphor for sorrow, now became a cleansing force, washing away the fear that had gripped his heart.

As the rain intensified, Riley leaned in, capturing Alex's lips in a gentle kiss. It was a silent rebellion against the judgments that lingered in the shadows. In that stolen moment, beneath Veridian's weeping sky, they vowed to face the storm hand in hand.

The news of their public display of affection rippled through the city, triggering a mix of reactions. While some celebrated the love that dared to defy societal norms, others clung to their prejudices, refusing to embrace the changing tides.

In the midst of the storm, Alex and Riley found strength in their shared umbrella, metaphorical and literal. With every step they took together, soaked in the rain of both adversity and love, they became a testament to the resilience of hearts unafraid to beat in sync with their own rhythm.

NAVIGATING LOVE'S LANDSCAPE

Veridian, now a canvas painted with both admiration and disapproval, became the backdrop for Alex and Riley's journey. Their love story, once a quiet melody, had transformed into a bold symphony echoing through the city's streets.

As they navigated the challenges of a love that dared to be different, Alex and Riley sought refuge in the places that had witnessed the birth of their connection. The bookstore, with its comforting scent of aged pages, became a sanctuary where they could retreat from the judgmental gazes that lingered outside.

They also discovered a haven in the hidden corners of the city, where acceptance bloomed like wildflowers. A community of artists, writers, and free spirits embraced their love, celebrating the courage it took to stand against the prevailing norms.

Yet, within this landscape of acceptance, shadows still loomed. The city's dichotomy – a blend of conservative traditions and progressive aspirations – mirrored the complexities within Alex and Riley's relationship.

Amidst the challenges, they found strength in each other. Alex's quiet determination complemented Riley's exuberant spirit, creating a balance that weathered the storms of judgment. Their love, like Veridian's ever-changing lights, flickered and danced, resilient in the face of adversity.

One evening, as they wandered through Veridian's art district, they stumbled upon an exhibition dedicated to celebrating unconventional love stories. The walls adorned with paintings and photographs depicted the myriad expressions of love that transcended societal norms.

Inspired by the vibrant display, Alex turned to Riley. "Our love is part of something bigger, something that challenges the status quo. Let's embrace it, Riley."

Riley, his eyes reflecting a mixture of gratitude and determination, nodded. "Veridian may have its critics, but it also has those who understand the beauty of love in all its forms. Let's focus on them."

Encouraged by the acceptance within the art community, Alex and Riley decided to share their story with a wider audience. They collaborated on an art project that illustrated the journey of their love amidst Veridian's changing landscapes. The project, titled

"Love Unveiled," aimed to challenge stereotypes and foster understanding.

As news of their collaborative venture spread, the city witnessed a shift in perception. Veridian, once divided by judgments, now faced a choice — to embrace the diversity of love or to resist the changing tides.

In the chapters that unfolded, Alex and Riley continued to navigate the complex landscape of love. Veridian, with its ever-evolving hues, mirrored the resilience of their connection. The city that once whispered judgments now hummed with a melody of acceptance, a testament to the transformative power of love that refused to be confined within the boundaries of societal expectations.

DANCING UNDER THE MOONLIGHT

Veridian, now a canvas painted with both admiration and disapproval, became the backdrop for Alex and Riley's journey. Their love story, once a quiet melody, had transformed into a bold symphony echoing through the city's streets.

As they navigated the challenges of a love that dared to be different, Alex and Riley sought refuge in the places that had witnessed the birth of their connection. The bookstore, with its comforting scent of aged pages, became a sanctuary where they could retreat from the judgmental gazes that lingered outside.

They also discovered a haven in the hidden corners of the city, where acceptance bloomed like wildflowers. A community of artists, writers, and free spirits embraced their love, celebrating the courage it took to stand against the prevailing norms.

Yet, within this landscape of acceptance, shadows still loomed. The city's dichotomy – a blend of conservative traditions and progressive aspirations – mirrored the complexities within Alex and Riley's relationship.

Amidst the challenges, they found strength in each other. Alex's quiet determination complemented Riley's exuberant spirit, creating a balance that weathered the storms of judgment. Their love, like Veridian's ever-changing lights, flickered and danced, resilient in the face of adversity.

One evening, as they wandered through Veridian's art district, they stumbled upon an exhibition dedicated to celebrating unconventional love stories. The walls adorned with paintings and photographs depicted the myriad expressions of love that transcended societal norms.

Inspired by the vibrant display, Alex turned to Riley. "Our love is part of something bigger, something that challenges the status quo. Let's embrace it, Riley."

Riley, his eyes reflecting a mixture of gratitude and determination, nodded. "Veridian may have its critics, but it also has those who understand the beauty of love in all its forms. Let's focus on them."

Encouraged by the acceptance within the art community, Alex and Riley decided to share their story with a wider audience. They collaborated on an art project that illustrated the journey of their love amidst Veridian's changing landscapes. The project, titled

"Love Unveiled," aimed to challenge stereotypes and foster understanding.

As news of their collaborative venture spread, the city witnessed a shift in perception. Veridian, once divided by judgments, now faced a choice — to embrace the diversity of love or to resist the changing tides.

In the chapters that unfolded, Alex and Riley continued to navigate the complex landscape of love. Veridian, with its ever-evolving hues, mirrored the resilience of their connection. The city that once whispered judgments now hummed with a melody of acceptance, a testament to the transformative power of love that refused to be confined within the boundaries of societal expectations.

DANCING UNDER THE MOONLIGHT II

Veridian began to transform, not just physically with the changing seasons but metaphorically, as the city's perception of Alex and Riley's love story evolved. The once-muted whispers of judgment were gradually drowned out by the resonating melody of acceptance.

Embracing this shift, Alex and Riley decided to take another bold step – sharing their love with the city in a way that transcended words. The city's central plaza, adorned with twinkling lights and the gentle hum of night life, became the stage for an unexpected dance under the moonlight.

One evening, Veridian gathered to witness a performance that was as much a celebration of love as it was a testament to courage. Alex, dressed in understated elegance, and Riley, donning an outfit that reflected the vibrancy of his spirit, took their place in the center of the plaza.

As the music began, the couple moved with a synchronicity that mirrored the harmony of their love. The dance unfolded like a story, each movement an expression of the challenges they had faced and the triumphs they had achieved together.

Their performance wasn't just a dance; it was a declaration. A declaration of love that refused to be confined by societal norms. A declaration that resonated with those who had faced similar struggles and sought solace in the possibility of love without boundaries.

The crowd, initially curious, soon found themselves captivated by the beauty of the dance. The rhythmic steps and graceful twirls seemed to cast a spell, uniting Veridian in a shared moment of acceptance and celebration.

As the music reached its crescendo, Alex and Riley embraced in a finale that echoed the depth of their connection. The applause that followed wasn't just for a captivating dance; it was a collective acknowledgment of love's ability to transcend preconceived notions.

The plaza, once a witness to hushed judgments, now echoed with cheers and claps. Veridian, as if applauding the courage displayed by its residents, illuminated the night with a kaleidoscope of lights, creating a backdrop for a love story that had become an integral part of the city's narrative.

In the aftermath of their moonlit dance, Alex and Riley walked hand in hand through the plaza. Their journey, marked by challenges and triumphs, continued. Veridian, with its ever-changing hues, seemed to embrace their love as an integral thread in the rich tapestry of the city's stories.

As they disappeared into the city's nocturnal embrace, the moonlight lingered, casting its glow on a city that had learned to dance to the rhythm of acceptance. The pages of their love story, now interwoven with Veridian's own narrative, turned with the promise of more chapters yet to be written.

EPHEMERAL ETERNITY

Veridian, having witnessed the evolution of Alex and Riley's love, now held their story within its beating heart. The city had become a silent ally, a backdrop for a love that defied conventions, and as the final chapter of their tale unfolded, it was time for the couple to reflect on their journey.

Amidst the quiet charm of "Whispers of the Page," Alex and Riley found a moment of respite. The bookstore, once a haven for Alex's solitude, had transformed into a symbol of the enduring strength of their love. Surrounded by the familiar scent of aged pages, they exchanged glances that spoke volumes.

"Who would have thought our story would become a part of Veridian's legacy?" Riley mused, his eyes reflecting the countless emotions they had weathered together.

Alex smiled, a blend of nostalgia and contentment. "Our journey was unexpected, but every twist and turn brought us closer. Veridian became more than just a city; it became the canvas upon which our love story unfolded."

As they reminisced about the challenges they had faced – the whispers, the judgments, and the moonlit dance that changed everything – Veridian, with its ever-changing lights, seemed to echo their sentiment. The city's skyline glowed in hues of acceptance, a visual ode to the transformative power of love.

Their reflections were interrupted by a gentle rain that began to fall outside. It was as if Veridian itself was shedding tears – tears of joy for a love that had triumphed over adversity.

In that quiet moment, with the rain as their witness, Alex turned to Riley. "Our love is like the rain – gentle, yet capable of washing away the doubts and prejudices that once clouded our path."

Riley's eyes gleamed with understanding. "And like the rain, our love is essential for growth and renewal. Veridian changed with us, adapting to the rhythm of our story."

As they stood together, hand in hand, the rain outside intensified. Veridian, now fully bathed in the cleansing embrace of the storm, seemed to echo the couple's sentiments – a city that celebrated the ephemeral yet eternal nature of love.

The final chapter of their story was written in the rain-kissed pages of Veridian. As they stepped into the city's nocturnal embrace, Alex and Riley knew that their love story, intertwined with the ever-evolving narrative of Veridian, would endure in the collective memory of a city that had learned to cherish love in all its beautiful forms.

And so, as Veridian's lights flickered in the rain-soaked night, the story of Alex and Riley became a part of the city's lore – a testament to the enduring power of love that, despite the storms it faced, painted the canvas of Veridian with hues of acceptance, resilience, and the promise of a future where love could thrive without fear.

About the Author

YourTimeless Writer

He is YourTimeless Writer, a third-year college student taking Bachelor in secondary education, Major in English. He discovered his love for writing since when he is in high school, but only on the late 2023 that he made a move on his love for writing. He wrote short stories and poems based from his experiences and observations which leads him creating one of his works, Whispers of the Heart. This future teacher is in to music, beside from writing, he loves to sing and dance too. Which add colors to his creativity for creating different stories and poems.

www.ingramcontent.com/pod-product-compliance
Lightning Source LLC
LaVergne TN
LVHW041643070526
838199LV00053B/3533